Pansy

Gertrude's Diary

Pansy

Gertrude's Diary

ISBN/EAN: 9783337192020

Printed in Europe, USA, Canada, Australia, Japan

Cover: Foto ©Andreas Hilbeck / pixelio.de

More available books at **www.hansebooks.com**

FOUR OF US.

GERTRUDE'S DIARY

AND

THE CUBE

BY

PANSY

Author of "Christie's Christmas," "An Endless Chain,"
"Esther Ried Yet Sreaking," "Hall in the
Grove," "Four Girl's at Chautauqua,"
"New Year's Tangles," etc.

BOSTON
LOTHROP PUBLISHING COMPANY

PANSY

TRADE-MARK REGISTERED JUNE 4, 1885.

GERTRUDE'S DIARY

WE BELIEVE THAT
THROUGH THE GRACE
OF THE LORD JESUS CHRIST,
WE SHALL BE SAVED, EVEN AS
THEY.

BE YE DOERS OF THE WORD,
AND NOT HEARERS ONLY.

BY THY WORDS THOU SHALT BE JUSTIFIED, AND BY THY
WORDS THOU SHALT BE CONDEMNED.

HUMBLE YOURSELVES IN THE SIGHT OF THE LORD, AND
HE SHALL LIFT YOU UP.

THERE are four of us, Ruth, and Namie, and
Prissy, and I. We are most always together,
and what one does, the others want to. Ruth
and Namie are sisters. Naomi, the name is,
but we always say Namie for short. I told

7

mother I thought it was funny that two sisters
should be named Ruth and Naomi after the
Bible, but mother said it seemed natural to her.
That Ruth was such a sweet character it would
be pleasant to a mother to name her little girl
for her, and that when she had a sister, Ruth's
sister Naomi would come to mind, of course.
So I don't know but it is natural, as mother
says; but I wouldn't like to be named Naomi
unless I could do better than Naomi Bible did.
I don't think much of her.   Prissy's real name
is Priscilla Morgan Henderson. Of course we
never say that.   Everybody calls her just
Prissy.   Ruth can't be nicknamed, and she
says she is glad of it ; but I could be.   My name
is Gertrude Morrison.   Nobody ever thinks of
calling me Gertie, or Gert, as they do with that
Loomis girl.   I am Gertrude to everybody.
Mother says she began that way; that she
doesn't like the fashion of clipping girls' names,
as though people never had time to call them
just what they are; but I think I should sort of
like to be called Gertie.   It sounds sweet — but
then, I am hardly ever sweet, so I suppose it
wouldn't fit.

Well, we are going to keep a diary, we four.

We are to write in it every day, and are to put the golden texts at the beginning of each month, as measures for us to measure our days by.

Mr. Neale told us that. We think it is a real queer idea; and Prissy says she guesses there will be some funny measuring, but we like to do it, after all. We like everything that Mr. Neale says. He is our minister, and he is nice and pleasant. We don't think of being afraid of him, though the first Sunday he had our class we all thought we should faint. He has it often now — once a month. Miss Archer, our teacher, goes home once a month and stays over Sunday, and Mr. Neale takes her place. He doesn't think it is nice for a teacher to go away once a month and leave her class, but we girls do; we wish she would go home every Sunday, and leave us to Mr. Neale.

We are to tell him how we get on measuring our days. I said I didn't believe I would have a thing to tell; but I've found out already some things I might tell if I wanted to, only I'm sure I don't.

This afternoon my sister Frank was getting her French exercise ready, and she had to translate this verse into French:

" Whose adorning let it not be that outward
adorning of plaiting the hair, or of wearing of
gold, or of putting on of apparel, but let it be
the hidden man of the heart, in that which is
not corruptible, even the ornament of a meek
and quiet spirit, which is in the sight of God of
great price."

She brought her French Bible to me, and I
had to watch while she read her translation, to
see if she had it right. She made some mis-
takes, and we had to go over it two or three
times before she got it to suit her.

Well, a little while afterwards I was dressing
to go to our Mission Band, and I wanted to wear
my garnet dress and mother did not want me to.
She said it was too much dressed just to go
over to Namie's with a few little girls, but I had
set my heart on wearing it, and I coaxed and
coaxed, and when I found that did no good, I
slammed the door as hard as I could, and I
jerked my blue dress so hard in getting it down
from the hook that it tore a little speck; and I
said that I never could wear anything decent,
but always had to go looking like a fright! It
sounds horrid to write them down here, but
those were just the words I said. Just then

Frank began to read over her lesson to mother, about not being particular about putting on costly apparel, and all that. It made me feel kind of ashamed, and I stopped talking to my blue dress, and hurried as fast as I could and went away to the Mission Band.

I never once thought anything about its having anything to do with these verses until this evening, when I opened my diary. Then the first verse I saw staring at me was that, "Be ye doers of the word and not hearers only." I do think it was strange! There I had been hearing that word about dressing, and keeping a quiet spirit, and all that, and then I went and did right the other thing.

Ruth said this afternoon that her actions were all too short; they wouldn't fit the measure at all. I didn't know what she meant, but I begin to understand.

I wouldn't tell Mr. Neale about this for anything.

Jan. 21st.— Something happens almost every day, and it is a good deal as Ruth says. Things are too short. To-day the baby had a new picture book — lovely colored pictures — and she sat down in the corner to have a good time,

But what did she do with almost every leaf she turned but pucker up her pretty little mouth and say: "Oh, dood dracious!" It sounded so funny that I wanted to laugh, but mother looked very grave, and kept telling baby that she must not say so; it was naughty. At last, she told her if she said it again the book would be taken from her. For about five minutes baby remembered, then she turned to a very bright picture, and out came the words again: "Dood dracious!" Mother came and took the book away, and baby cried hard enough to break my heart, but as soon as she could speak she sobbed out: "Dertrude says so. She said it to her hair all the time." Then I remembered that this morning when I was combing my hair it pulled and snarled dreadfully, and I suppose I must have said the words without thinking. Mother looked at me very soberly, and told me I would do well to look in my diary and see how true one of my texts was. I couldn't think what she meant, and I felt ashamed to ask her; yet here it is: "By thy words thou shalt be condemned." And it seems my naughty words condemned baby too. Oh, dear me! I should think I would learn to be careful.

Jan. 30th.— To-day Ruth had something that "measured." We had a spelling-down school. It was great fun. I stood up a good while, and at last I got down on a silly little word of two syllables. I shall always know how to spell sulphur after this, but I couldn't believe it possible that there was any other way than " sulpher." I had two chances, and spelled it the same each time, because it did not seem to me that there could be any other way. Well, pretty soon the word "separate" came to Ruth. There were only three standing then, and Ruth was our particular friend, and we did hope she would stand the longest, so we all nodded our heads at her to encourage her. She smiled, and spelled. "Right," said Miss Belmont, and she smiled pleasantly; "so many boys and girls spell that word incorrectly that I am particularly glad you made no mistake."

Ralph Burns, who is always talking, asked how they spelled it, and Miss Belmont said, " With an e."

Just then there was a knock at the door, and one of the professors wanted to speak to Miss Belmont; and she was gone quite a few minutes. We girls kept bowing and smiling at Ruth, so

glad that she had not been beaten, but she looked
real sober. When Miss Belmont came back, she
spoke real quick as if she was in a hurry to get
the words said:

"Miss Belmont, I spelled that word with an
'e.' I thought that was the way."

Miss Belmont looked astonished, and we girls
looked disgusted, and Prissy said she was sure
Ruth was mistaken, that she heard the "a" just
as plain as day. But Ruth kept saying that she
knew she spelled it with an "e," that she had
not thought of there being any other way; so
she went and sat down.

Ralph Burns stood up the longest, but it
wasn't very long, and he told Miss Belmont that
he should have got down on "separate," if it
had come to him, for he always spelled it with
an "e." I thought that was real nice of him.
Right after spelling, we had recess.

We asked Ruth what she corrected Miss Belmont's mistake for; that we didn't think it was
necessary. And Ruth said yes, it was; it wasn't
being humble in the sight of the Lord to take
praise that did not belong to you. She said that
softly to me, for she knew I would remember
the verse, and I did.

"Ruth," I said to her, "you did the first part of the verse, but you haven't had the last happen to you."

"Yes, I have," she said. "I feel 'lifted up' in my heart, and real happy."

It was real queer, but the last part of the verse came true right before our eyes. It was about three o'clock, and we all sat there studying, when the door opened and Professor Thompson looked in.

"Miss Belmont," he said, "if you have a young lady here whom you are sure you can trust to do just as she is told, and to tell a thing just as it is, I want to borrow her for a little while to drive with me to town."

And Miss Belmont said she believed there were a good many of her girls whom she could recommend, but just now the one that she was sure of was Miss Ruth Chester.

We don't know what he wanted, nor anything about it, but we know she rode away in Professor Thompson's sleigh, and it is a very handsome one, all lined with red, and with lovely soft robes; and he drives two splendid horses, and the bells are just lovely. They went to town too, and did not get back until most dark, for I saw the sleigh dash by awhile ago; and of course Ruth had a splendid time—people who go with Professor Thompson always do. Miss Janie Thompson and Mr. Will Thompson went too; and they are just as splendid as they can be! I think it was real queer how Ruth got "lifted up" right away.

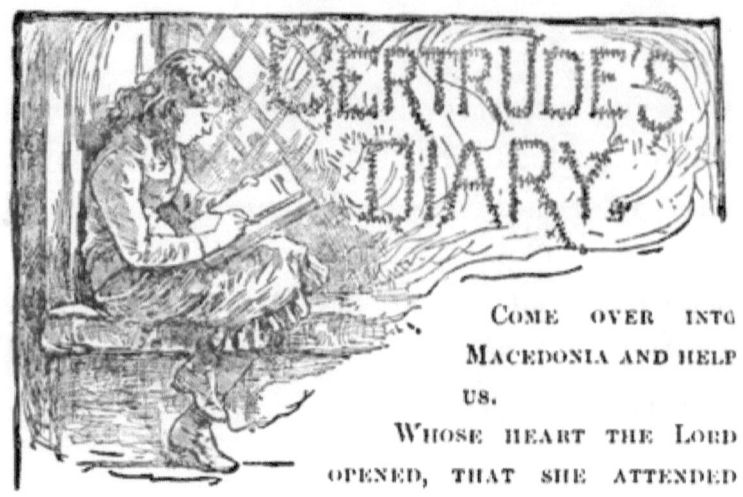

COME OVER INTO MACEDONIA AND HELP US.

WHOSE HEART THE LORD OPENED, THAT SHE ATTENDED UNTO THE THINGS WHICH WERE SPOKEN OF PAUL. BELIEVE ON THE LORD JESUS CHRIST, AND THOU SHALT BE SAVED, AND THY HOUSE.

THESE WERE MORE NOBLE THAN THOSE IN THESSALONICA, IN THAT THEY RECEIVED THE WORD WITH ALL READINESS OF MIND AND SEARCHED THE SCRIPTURES DAILY WHETHER THOSE THINGS WERE SO.

MONDAY:— I don't believe in Macedonia, but we had a talk last night about the Bible verses where Paul was called to go there and help the people. I told mother I thought it

17

would have been real nice to have lived in those
times, and be called in dreams to go to places and
do things. Of course she said people were just
as much called now, and of course I know they
are, but it doesn't seem the same, and I said so.
I said if an angel should speak to me and tell me
to do a thing, I was sure I would do it.

I suppose that was what made me dream of
the Scanlon children. They are the horridest
looking children, dirty and ragged and half wild!
They live at the end of the lane where we girls
cut across sometimes for short, and I always put
my hand up to my face so I won't smell any of
their queer smells, and rush by as fast as I can.

Well, last night I dreamed that Mr. Neale
came and stood right by my chair while I was
getting my arithmetic lesson. I looked up at
him and all at once he changed into one of the
Scanlon children, and said :

"Come over into Pine Alley and help us."
Then he vanished, and I awoke, and mother was
at the foot of the stairs, calling me to hurry up
and do an errand for her.

I could not get this dream out of my thoughts,
and at recess I told the girls. They all thought
it was queer. The more we talked about it,

the more we all thought that maybe there was something we ought to do for the Scanlons.

On the way home we met Mr. Neale, and Prissy, who is never afraid of anybody, told him about my dream.

"That's a good dream," he said. "It means that you are to try to get Phil Scanlon to sign the pledge and take care of his family; and the children are to be coaxed into the Sabbath-school."

We looked at one another, and Namie giggled. She said afterwards she would most as soon think of coaxing little pigs into Sunday-school.

After Mr. Neale went away, we all talked at once. We said we never could, and there was no use in trying, anyway; that everybody knew that nothing could be done for the Scanlons. I said I was afraid of Phil Scanlon and always ran when I saw him staggering along; and I don't believe my mother would let me speak to him.

Ruth said she should like well enough to get the children into Sunday-school, but they hadn't anything decent to wear. At last we made up a plan to try for the children. We meant to go around to our different mothers, and some other mothers, and get some clothes for them, and then give them to them if they would promise to come to Sunday-school. I don't know whether we can do anything or not, but we mean to try.

Tuesday:— Don't you believe, you dear old journal, that he has done it! Old Phil has, I mean. I was never so astonished in my life. I have thought about him a good deal ever since that dream. Whenever I passed the lane I would think how that voice sounded that said : " Come over into Pine Alley and help us!"

On Sunday we had a temperance lesson, and Mr. Neale presented us each with a little red pledge book and asked us to get all the signers we could.

I thought of Phil Scanlon right away, and I did wish somebody would get him. That night I prayed that God would send somebody to coax him to sign the pledge ; for they say he is a real decent man when he is sober, and that Mrs. Scanlon used to be nice, when she had anything to be nice with. All the time I thought I wouldn't go near him because I was afraid ; I thought I wouldn't speak to him for anything. Last night I wouldn't go through the alley for fear I should see him. I went away around by

Duane street; but I was thinking about him all the time, and I kept praying that God would do something for him,

Well, when I turned the corner of Duane street, there stood Phil Scanlon right by the saloon, one foot on the step, going in. My heart seemed to hop right into my mouth. I didn't think I was going to speak a word, but I did; I said: "I wish you wouldn't go in there, Mr. Scanlon." I never heard him called Mr. Scanlon in my life, but of course it wouldn't have been polite for me to say Phil.

He turned around and looked at me, and said: "What in thunder do you wish that for? What business is it to you?"

I don't know about it's being right to put that word 'thunder' in my diary, but that is just what he said.

I was scared, but I spoke up quickly: "It is a good deal to me, and to lots of people; we want you to sign the pledge and have nice clothes and hot things to eat, and send Carrie and little Phil to school. Everybody says your little Phil is real smart, and ought to go to school."

"Who told you to say all this to me?" That

was what he asked me, and his voice was so cross it frightened me so that my teeth chattered. But when he asked me who told me, it made me think of my dream, and all at once I thought what if God really did mean me to understand from that dream that I was to try to help those Scanlons? "I don't know but God did," said I. "I had a dream about it, and I think maybe he sent me."

Then Phil Scanlon kind of laughed, and said: "It must have been somebody from another world; for nobody in this one cared what became of him."

Well, I hardly know how it all was, but I got out my pledge book and showed him. I hadn't a single signer, and I told him I would like to have his name the first on the list. I don't know what made him do it, I didn't believe he would, and everybody thinks it is the strangest thing; but he signed the pledge!

"PHILIP SCANLON."

It is real nice writing. I've showed it to ever so many people, and they are real interested in him, and are going to help him all they can.

When I showed it to Mr. Neale and said I couldn't think what made him sign, he smiled and said : " Whose heart the Lord opened, that he attended unto the things which were spoken by Gertrude."

Friday :— We girls have had such fun ! We have organized a society ; we call ourselves the " B. R. N." The boys can't find out what it means, and we don't intend to tell them yet awhile, anyway. What it really does mean is, the " Bible Reading Nobility." Mr. Neale put it into our minds by pointing out how much more noble those folks in Berea were than the ones in Thessalonica ; and then he said there was a chance for boys and girls to be noble in the same way.

That gave us our plan, and we organized, the very next afternoon. We read the Bible together for a half-hour every day. We each have a blank book, and we take notes, and at the close read our notes aloud. It is real nice. I didn't know before that the Bible was so interesting.

IN HIM WE LIVE, AND MOVE, AND HAVE OUR BEING.

I AM WITH THEE, AND NO MAN SHALL SET ON THEE TO HURT THEE: FOR I HAVE MUCH PEOPLE IN THIS CITY.

FOR IF WE BELIEVE THAT JESUS DIED AND ROSE AGAIN, EVEN SO THEM ALSO WHICH SLEEP IN JESUS WILL GOD BRING WITH HIM.

BE NOT WEARY IN WELL DOING.

WE have had a strange time, we girls; I have been so busy that I could not write in my diary, and now I don't know where to commence.

In the first place we quarrelled with Anna

Dudley. That isn't strange; you see we are always quarrelling with her, or she is with us; I don't know as there can be a more disagreeable girl than she has been. But that isn't right; I didn't mean to say it. If it were not for spoiling a page in my diary, I would tear it out.

We hadn't spoken to Anna in three days and we said we never would have anything more to do with her. Then her little baby sister got sick, and one day she died! We were just as sorry for Anna as we could be, for the baby was so sweet and cunning! She was two years old, and one day Anna brought her to school, and she kissed us all.

We got together and talked it up, and said we ought to go and see Anna, but we did not want to, for we couldn't think of anything to say to her.

We asked Mr. Neale about it, and he told us to do just what we thought we would like to have Anna do, if we were in her place; and at last we said we would go.

On the way we tried to think of something to say, and we made up two or three things that sounded nice, only none of us wanted to say them. At last Ruthie said : "Girls, let's just kiss her and not say anything."

And that is just what we did. She came down to see us, and we each went up and kissed her, and Prissy gave her a rosebud, and then she began to cry.

"You don't know how *she* loved flowers," she said, meaning her little baby sister. "She would pucker up her little nose to smell them whenever she saw any ; and oh, to think that I will never see her again ! "

Then she cried so hard, that all we could do was to cry too. Only what she said made me think of one of our verses, and I spoke right up before I thought : "Why, Anna," I said, "you will see her again, you know. She 'sleeps in Jesus.' He said, ' Suffer the little ones to come unto me.' "

She stopped sobbing and looked at me. "When do you mean ?" she asked. "Why, when He comes. ' Even so, them also which sleep in Jesus will God bring with him.' When he comes after all his people he will bring Daisy along ; and then you will see her.' "

"That is so," she said. She remembered the verse, for she always learns her verses.

"But then, maybe I will be so afraid that I can't take any comfort with looking at her."

It seemed such a strange thing to say! I did not know how to answer her, but she looked right at me as though she thought I would. "I don't want to be afraid of Him when he comes," I said. It was all I could think of to say, and it was just what I meant. "I don't either," said Ruth; "my father will be along, you know, and I want to be glad to see him. Girls, we ought to get ready, so we would be sure not to be afraid. Just think how dreadful it would seem to have Daisy shouting out after us, and we so scared that we couldn't smile back on her!"

Well, we stayed quiet awhile and talked with Anna, and told her we were sorry for her, and she thanked us for coming to see her, and said she was sorry that she had acted so in school that last day. She said she was so worried about little Daisy then, that she couldn't help being cross. Then we kissed her and came away, and we all said we would try to be real good to Anna after this, and not quarrel with her any more. But to-day in school she was almost as cross as ever, and it was just the hardest work not to tell her she was too hateful for us to have anything to do with her! We all kept pretty still, but it was dreadfully hard work. Namie did say that we had one week of peace this term; she meant the week that Anna stayed out because Daisy was sick. She was sorry she said it, right away, and looked up quickly at Anna, but she had muttered it so that we think Anna did not hear.

I told mother about it to-night, and asked her if she didn't think it strange that Anna should be so cross after we had been good to her. All the answer she made was to ask me if there wasn't another verse on our card that would help us. So I read them all over carefully, after I came up-stairs, and I guess mother means:

"Be not weary in well doing."

GERTRUDE'S DIARY

AND WHEN PAUL HAD LAID HIS HANDS UPON THEM, THE HOLY GHOST CAME ON THEM.

AND MANY THAT BELIEVED, CAME AND CONFESSED AND SHOWED THEIR DEEDS. WE PREACH CHRIST CRUCIFIED, UNTO THE JEWS A STUMBLING-BLOCK, AND UNTO THE GREEKS FOOLISHNESS.

IF MEAT MAKE MY BROTHER TO OFFEND, I WILL EAT NO FLESH WHILE THE WORLD STANDETH.

I HAVE had just a dreadful time! I don't suppose I have behaved so badly since I was quite a little girl.

It all began with my brother Ben; or no, I don't suppose I ought to say that; it began in

29

my feeling a little bit vain over my diary. I
have tried to write very nicely in it. I print
the texts at the beginning of each month, and
father says I print beautifully, and everybody
says I am a very good writer for a girl of my
age. Ben writes badly because he is so careless;
one day mother, when she was looking at my
diary, said, "Ben ought to see this, Gertrude;
he never takes any pains with his writing."

So yesterday, when I had my diary down-stairs
and he wanted to see it, I opened to the first
page, because I thought there was nothing on it
that I would not be willing to have him read,
and I thought it looked a little bit better than
any of the others. Well, he began to read,
without saying a word about the writing or the
printing, and in a few minutes he burst out
laughing. Oh, he just shouted, and doubled
himself up, as if he had found something so
funny that he could not get over it.

I tried to get the book away from him, but
he held fast to it, and laughed: "Oh, ho, ho!
if this isn't rich! Ha, ha, ha! Mother, listen
to this, and see if you don't feel complimented."
And he began to read aloud from my diary.

I snatched the book then, in good earnest, and

got it; but he went on laughing, and mother laughed a little too, and I didn't see yet what it was all about, until Ben said:

"So your Bible made Ruth and Naomi into sisters, eh? If that isn't queer; oh no, it wasn't the Bible, it was mother. Why, mother! the idea of your not knowing that they were mother and daughter! Won't that be a jolly thing to tell the boys!" and he went to doubling himself up again, and laughing as though it was the funniest thing in the world. Then I saw for the first time that I had written in my diary as though those two people were sisters, when of course I knew better all the time. I always knew what relation they were, just as well as Ben did; and of course I did not mean that mother said any such thing. What I meant to say was, that when Ruth came to have a sister, it was natural that they should think of Naomi, whom Ruth loved so much that she followed her home; and there I had gone and said that nonsense. It was real silly, of course, but I didn't see any sense in Ben making such a time about it. Mother only laughed a little, and when she saw it troubled me, she said: "Ben, I am ashamed of you." But that boy kept re-

peating the sentence, and adding all sorts of
funny thoughts to it, and laughing as though he
would never get over it, and making believe that
he thought I did not know any better, until I
thought I should fly. I burst right out, at last,
crying and talking at the same time. I said I
thought he was the meanest boy there ever was
in this world; and that I would never show
him anything again, nor have anything to do
with him. And I stamped my foot, and oh,
acted awfully! Ben stopped laughing, and
looked surprised, but I rushed right on, until
father spoke to me from the next room. I did
not know he was there. He just spoke my
name, and not another word. After a minute,
he said to Ben:

"Perhaps you would do well to keep a diary,
my son, and write that verse in it about stum-
bling-blocks. You are not the first one whom
I have seen use a little knowledge for others to
stumble over."

Well, then I felt ashamed all through me. It
made me think of my verses and my resolutions,
and how I had broken them.

But I did not get over being angry at Ben;
I would not look at him, even after he said to

father, " I didn't mean any harm, sir; I was just
having a little fun with Gertrude. I did not
suppose she would fly into a passion."

Fly into a passion, indeed, when he had
made me stumble into it, right over him! I
thought what father said was good for him;
but for all that, I was so sorry I had stumbled.
I ran away up to my room and hid you, my dear
diary, in a drawer, and said I would never
write in you as long as I lived. And then I sat
down in a little heap on the foot of the bed and
cried. I had meant to have such nice times with
Ben, and now they are all spoiled That was
two hours ago, and I have not spoken to him
since, and don't mean to. He need not have
been so mean. I wouldn't have acted that way
for anything. I have made up my mind to try
again, and to write in my diary as usual; but I
will let Ben alone for the rest of this vacation.

Evening.— Oh, dear! I wish I had not written all that in my diary. I wonder if diaries
are real nice? You are always writing in them
what you wish you hadn't, and then having to
take it back. After I had that dreadful time
this morning, I did not feel happy a bit.

I went down to dinner, but I did not speak to

Ben, only when I had to answer a question, and then I spoke as short as I could, and did not look at him at all. When I sat with mother at my mending in the afternoon, she asked me if I did not feel willing to forgive Ben, after he had said that he did not mean any harm. I told her I meant to forgive him, but as for talking with him any more I did not want to; that he had been real mean, and led me into doing what was wrong; that he had been a stumbling-block to me, just as father said.

"He is three years older than you," mother said, and I thought that was queer.

It couldn't be right to treat me in that way, just because he was older. I said, " I thought there was less excuse for him on that account; that he ought to have been even more careful about making me stumble."

"I didn't suppose you thought so," mother said. "I had reason to suppose you would think it all right, as soon as you remembered the difference in your ages."

Well, I laid down the stocking I was darning, and looked at her; I could not imagine what she meant, and I told her so.

"Why," she said, "I heard you making all

manner of sport of Charlie the other day because he thought that Boston was in Maine, and he is four years younger than you. You certainly made him stumble sadly that day, and I supposed your excuse would be that you were older than he and had a right to laugh at him."

And there I was! I had done just as mean a thing to poor Charlie, and thought nothing of it ; and Charlie had forgiven me in less than an hour, and came and kissed me good-night as sweetly as possible! Oh, dear! I didn't say another word to mother, but finished my stocking as fast as I could, and went to my room. I am not going to show my diary to anybody any more; so I will tell you that I prayed three times before I felt like treating Ben just as though nothing had happened. Then I brought out my diary and was going to write down what I meant to do, and there was that verse about how the people came and confessed. I said aloud:

"Oh, I never can! I'll treat him just as usual, but I don't want to tell him that I think I have been a goose, and that I have treated little Charlie exactly as he has me." But it didn't do any good. There was no getting away from that verse.

At last I went down, and found Ben out in the carriage house, and I told him the whole story from beginning to end. As soon as he could get a chance to speak, he said, " All right, Gertrude, I was as mean as dirt; but I didn't mean to be, really, and I won't do it again. Let's go and take a ride together."

And we did, and had a nice time. Now that I have come up here to my room for the night, it doesn't seem to me as though Ben did any-thing very bad, after all. It was mean in me to tease Charlie, because he is such a little fellow; but, of course, Ruth and Naomi were not sisters —I mean Bible Ruth and Naomi were not — and of course I knew it; and I suppose Ben thought I would have sense enough to laugh over the mistake with him. Why can't people think about things at the time, as they will five hours afterwards, I wonder.

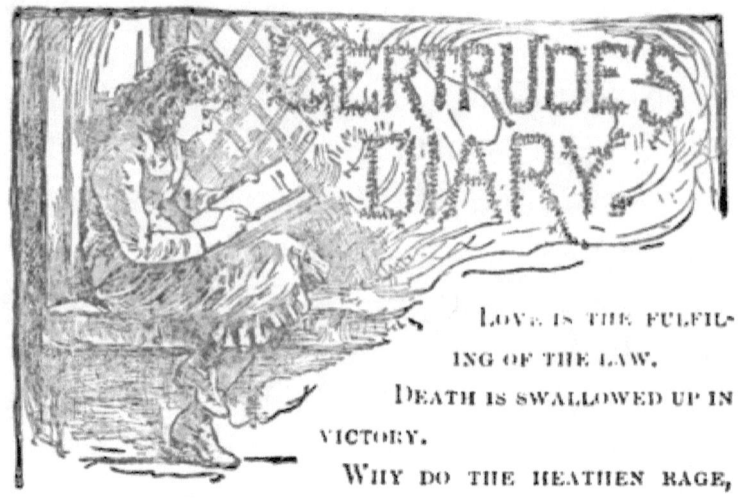

LOVE IS THE FULFIL-
ING OF THE LAW.
DEATH IS SWALLOWED UP IN
VICTORY.
WHY DO THE HEATHEN RAGE,
AND THE PEOPLE IMAGINE A VAIN THING?
GOD LOVETH A CHEERFUL GIVER.

I THINK it is just dreadful, anyway, that folks all know such a little bit about themselves, and about the way they are going to act. We had a real mean time at the Society this afternoon, and it was all my fault, and it was at our house, too. It is the B. R. N. Society; we can't read the Bible all the time, and we like to

37

be together, so we planned to sew things that
would help people. Ruth thought of it; she
said that the name " B. R. N." would fit us,
because it would not do people any good to read
the Bible unless they practised it, and to make
things for poor folks would be practising.

Then Prissy, who always wants to know all
about everything, asked where in the Bible it
told us to sew for folks? And Ruth said that
the verse we all recited in school the day before
told it. The verse was: " Whatsoever thy
hand findeth to do, do it with thy might."
Ruth said she was sure that our hands had found
this sewing to do. We laughed at her a little
for always finding a verse in the Bible to prove
that her way was right; but she does know more
about the Bible than any of the rest of us do.

Well, we went to work, hemming aprons for
the little Scanlon children. For we still keep
thinking about them. It seems as though they
never *would* get put in order. Their father
keeps his pledge, and he works real hard; but
there is such a large family, and everything was
so ragged and dirty, and the furniture all gone.
Mother says if they were all started new with
furniture and clothes and everything, it would

take as much as the father could earn to keep
them in food and clothes.

So we girls are going to try to help them get
started new; our mothers gave us some nice
pretty calico, and Prissy's mother cut out ever
so many aprons — nice large ones which cover
people all up; why, they are just like little Gabri-
elle dresses, only they have no lining, and they
can be put on over another dress; my mother
sewed the long seams on the machine, and fixed
the hems, and we were all at work this afternoon
as nice as could be, and we were talking about
that little Gertie Scanlon. She is lame and cannot walk a step, and she is a real sweet-looking
little girl and doesn't have any pleasures. We
all said we felt sorry for her, and wished we
could do something extra for her. Then Namie
squealed right out: "O Gertrude Morrison, I
know something perfectly splendid! You can
give her your little carriage; she would just fit
into it real nicely, and her little brother Dick is
real good to her; he could take her out riding
every day. Wouldn't that be nice! She is
your namesake, too, so it happens all right."

Now my carriage is the cunningest little thing!
I used to have it when I was small, and it is

cushioned with red leather, and has curtains, and is just a beauty. Of course I can't ride in it any more, but I keep it to play with when little children come to see us, and I have great fun taking the dolls out to ride, and well— I think everything of it. I felt just as mad at Namie as I could, and my face grew red, and I spoke right out:

"Oh, indeed, Miss Namie Chester! It is very easy for you to find things for other folks to give. Why wouldn't it be splendid for you to give her your great doll that came from Paris? I would thank you to pick out your own gifts and let mine alone!" Was there ever anything so hateful? I don't know what made me talk so, unless it was because I knew I ought to give that carriage away, and felt as though I *couldn't*, and tried to get away from it by being angry and talking loud.

The girls all looked astonished, and Ruth told Namie that she ought not to meddle, and then Namie cried and said she was sure she did not know she was doing any harm; that if the carriage were hers, she would give it in a minute. That made me feel more angry than before, and I told her it was easy enough for persons to tell what they would do, but I thought, for my part, it would be better to *do* some of it. Just then mother came into the room, and I said :

"Mother, what do you think Namie Chester wants me to do ? Give my little red-cushioned carriage to Gertie Scanlon. Do you think I had better ?"

Now I thought I was pretty sure that mother would not be willing to have me give it away, and if I had said so in the first place instead of getting angry, there wouldn't have been any fuss. Mother spoke real quietly, as she always does, and said :

"No, Gertrude ; I don't think so."

I turned to Namie with a nod of triumph, and never minded that she was crying, and feeling dreadfully; I began to say : "There, Namie Chester, you see you don't know everything, and"— And just then mother finished her sentence : "I don't think it would be a very acceptable gift, for ' The Lord loveth a cheerful giver.'" Then she walked out of the room.

I felt hot all over, and so ashamed that I wished I could slip down, out of sight. It was only yesterday that I had been telling the girls I thought that verse was easy enough to follow,

for I liked to give things; there was nothing I
enjoyed better. And I truly did not know until
this afternoon that I only liked to give away
the things which I did not want myself.

Friday.— I gave the carriage to Gertie Scanlon, and I did it real cheerfully, too. At first,
mother said I couldn't; and then I can't begin
to tell how I wanted to. It seemed to me that I
could never be happy again, if I could not do it.

One night mother came up to my room and
talked with me. She wanted to know what
made me so anxious now, when I was unwilling
before. I told her I truly thought it was because
I had seen how selfish I was to want to keep
that carriage for dolls, when it was large enough
for poor little Gertie to take rides in. Then
mother asked me if I had asked Namie Chester
to forgive me.

I said no, ma'am, I hadn't; that I could not
ask a little girl like her to forgive me, that I
would be ashamed to do so. Mother wanted to
know if I thought it would be wrong to ask her
— mothers do say such strange things! I said no,
of course not. And then she asked what there
would be to make me ashamed. Did I think
I had treated Namie properly? No, I didn't.

If some one had treated me improperly, would
I be more ashamed of them if they asked my
forgiveness, than I would if they kept silent?
I do think mothers are just the worst people to
ask questions! They stand you right up in
corners and you can't get away from them, no
matter how hard you try.

I did ask Namie to forgive me; and I told
her I was ashamed of myself; and she put her
arms around my neck, and said never mind.
And what do you think? She has actually
given Gertie Scanlon her Paris doll! She said
she never knew that she was selfish about it
until that day when I showed her she was.
She thinks she is getting too large to play with
dolls. But I am older than she, and I like to
play with them; and I don't think I could have
given away that doll. Mother says she doesn't
think Namie was called on to do it; that a
plainer doll would have done just as well for
little Gertie.

I suppose Namie would not have done it if
I had not made her uncomfortable; but then
Gertie hugs and kisses it, and takes it out riding
with her in her carriage, and says she is "most
too happy to live."

So some nice things come out of wrong things.

Dear me! It is a kind of a muddle. But I do wish I could learn to keep my temper. I don't believe I shall be angry with Namie again in a great while; perhaps never.

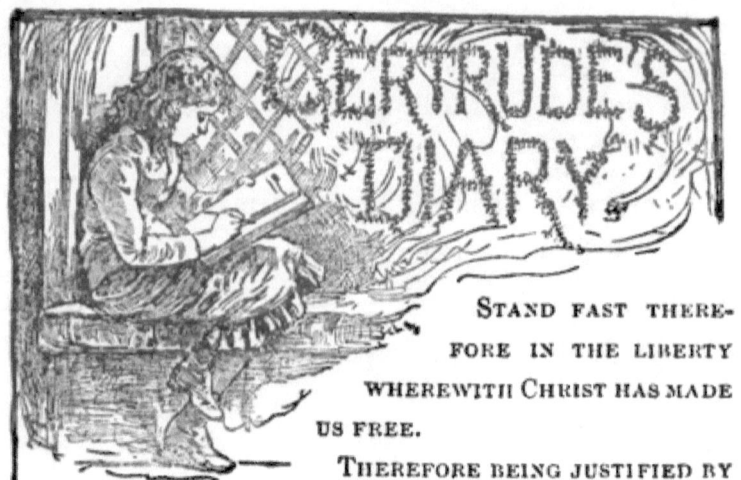

STAND FAST THERE-
FORE IN THE LIBERTY
WHEREWITH CHRIST HAS MADE
US FREE.

THEREFORE BEING JUSTIFIED BY
FAITH WE HAVE PEACE WITH GOD
THROUGH OUR LORD JESUS CHRIST.

WE KNOW THAT ALL THINGS WORK TOGETHER FOR GOOD
TO THEM THAT LOVE GOD.

LET EVERY SOUL BE SUBJECT UNTO THE HIGHER POWERS.

OTHER FOUNDATION CAN NO MAN LAY THAN THAT IS LAID,
WHICH IS JESUS CHRIST.

WE girls go to temperance meetings every single night. Mr. Ned Wilson who was here visiting last week said it was a queer time to have temperance meetings right in the middle of June; and our Tom who is real sharp some-

times asked him if people didn't drink whiskey
in the middle of June. Ned laughed, and said
he rather thought they did. After he went
away father said he was afraid that Ned knew
by experience that they did, for he was beginning to drink.

The temperance meetings are real splendid.
Great crowds come to them, and they sing a
great deal, and play on the organ, and the cor-
net, and ever so many go up and sign the pledge;
and Mr. Burdick talks; he is the temperance
lecturer. Oh, journal! I cannot help wishing
sometimes, that you were a girl and could enjoy
things, and talk back, you know. But, then, if
you could, I suppose you would talk right when
I wanted to, most everybody does, and I have
to keep still times when I am just as anxious to
speak as I can be. I guess it is better as it is.
I'll tell you: I am going to pretend that you *are*
a girl, but are deaf and dumb and I have to tell
you things in the sign language. Won't that be
nice.

The temperance meetings are not like any
that I ever attended before. Mr. Burdick talks
every night; he is just splendid. He has been
a drunkard; and while I don't suppose it can be

a good thing that this was so, still he does know more about the way they feel, and what will help them, than he could if he had never been one. Last night he told a story about a man who had reformed and he went to a house where they had peach sauce with brandy in it, and he ate some, without noticing the taste of brandy, and it made the awful thirst for liquor come back again, and he had to walk the floor for two nights, and pray. Mother does not put brandy in peaches, but she makes a kind of jelly that she puts wine in. I like it better than any jelly I ever tasted, and I didn't know there was wine in it until yesterday.

When I was helping her get dinner she told me about it, and said she: " Now, Gertrude, we have fifteen glasses of jelly with wine in it, and I suppose there is enough in it to affect a person, just as the peaches did that man about whom Mr. Burdick told. What do you think we would better do with it?"

Well, first I said I thought we ought to send it to Mrs. Akers, she is sick and poor, and it might strengthen her; then I thought of Harry Akers, he is fourteen and his mother always saves some of her good things for him; that

wouldn't do. Then I said the only safe place
I could think of for it was the garbage barrel.
Mother laughed and said she agreed with me,
and we had real fun putting it there. Tom
came home while we were doing it, and he
pretended he thought it was a dreadful waste ;
but last night he signed the pledge. He wouldn't
the night before, for he said he didn't want
to be tied with an apron string; that he knew
what was wrong to do, and could keep from
doing it without writing his name on a piece of
paper ; I asked him to-night what made him
change his mind, and he looked at me with a
queer laugh, and said, since the jelly was all
gone, he might as well sign as not. I don't
know what he meant. Mother says she never
knew before that a little wine used in cooking,
could do anybody any hurt.

But, my dear deaf and dumb friend, I was
going to tell you about one of the verses. We sat
together, last night, Ruth and Namie and I, and
Mr. Ned Wilson sat right behind us with two
other young men. He is Ruth's uncle. When
the people rushed up to sign the pledge, Ruth
leaned back and coaxed her uncle Ned to go
too. He laughed and said he couldn't, it was

against his principles. That sounded so queer that I asked him what it meant:

"Do you mean it is wrong to sign?" I asked him.

"Oh, no," he said, "there was nothing wrong about it for people who chose to do so, and who needed such crutches."

"But," I said, "I thought going against one's principles was wrong." And one of the young men bent forward to me and whispered:

"That depends, my little friend, on whether the principles in themselves are wrong or right, doesn't it?"

Now of course it does, but I had not thought of that. Still I did not understand it, and I asked Mr. Ned if he wouldn't tell me what he meant. He said he believed in people having liberty to do just as they pleased, or thought best, without being tied by a promise.

I asked him if that had anything to do with their promising not to do a thing that they didn't think best. Then those young men laughed; I am sure I don't know at what. The word "Liberty" made me think of one of our verses: "Stand fast therefore in the liberty wherewith Christ has made us free." And that made me think of our talk with Mr. Neale; we asked him what it meant and he explained, with a little silk thread. I said to Mr. Wilson that I thought the pledge was nothing but a little silk thread. He wanted to know what I meant, and kept questioning me, until he got the whole story. You see, we girls had almost quarrelled as to what the verse about liberty meant, and when Mr. Neale came in, we all rushed up to him to get help. He sat down right away and took a piece of strong twine from his pocket and asked me to break it. I tried, and tried, and it wouldn't break; then the girls tried, and they couldn't. Then he tied my hands with it, and told me to try to get free from it, and I couldn't. Then he asked mother for a spool of silk and she gave him a fine red silk. He took one thread of it and tied Namie's hands, and told her to break away; she did in a second. Then he tied Ruth with the same silk thread, and told her to hold still until he put up a sign. He printed on two cards two sentences: one said: " You are a slave." That he put in front of me. I laughed, but I told him it was true; I could not .get my hands free. The other card said: " If you break that thread you will grieve Jesus." This he put up before Ruth ; then when he told her to break the thread she shook her head and said : "I don't want to."

He smiled and said : "That is right, Ruthie, stand fast in the liberty wherewith Christ has made you free. You can, but you don't want to, for a grand reason."

Father says he thinks that this is a good illustration. Well, I had to tell it all off to Mr. Ned Wilson. He seemed a good deal interested, and don't you think to-night he signed the pledge! I don't suppose what I said had anything to do with it. Mr. Burdick talked about liberty to-night, and he made it so plain that I suppose Ned could not get away from it. When he came back from the pledge table, I was standing in the aisle waiting to let Mrs. Morse pass, and he whispered : "The thread of silk has got me, you see. I can, but I won't."

GERTRUDE'S DIARY

I HAVE FOUND DAVID MY SERVANT; WITH MY HOLY OIL HAVE I ANOINTED HIM.

HE BLESSETH THE HABITATION OF THE JUST.

THY THRONE SHALL BE ESTABLISHED FOREVER.

THINE OWN FRIEND, AND THY FATHER'S FRIEND, FORSAKE NOT.

IT was the meanest Fourth of July that I ever spent in my life! And we girls had been getting ready for it for more than a month, and thought it was going to be perfectly splendid!

The trouble was that Prissy and I quarrelled! I never thought we would, and it was all about such a silly little thing.

We were having our last rehearsal, the day before the Fourth. It was dreadfully warm up in the hall, and we were so tired we could hardly stand. We had been at work all day, trimming the hall, and rehearsing, and running of errands for the older folks, who never seem to think that the feet of girls younger than fourteen, *can* get tired !

Just as we were singing *Hail glorious Day !* for about the fourteenth time, I do believe — just because some of the girls would not put in the rest at the right place — Namie whispered to me that she should think they would all be glad to rest, if they were as tired as we. Well, right in the midst of it, Tom sent in word that he wanted to speak to me, and I had to be excused and go out to the hall, and down two flights of stairs, and all in the world he wanted was to know if I had seen his exercise book anywhere ! When I came back, Prissy had slipped into my chair. She knows I like to sit just there, and it is my place, for I have had it most every time. She did not make a motion toward moving when I came back; I was warm and tired, so I just nudged her and whispered : " Hurry up, and get out of my place."

She whispered back: "It is no more your place than mine," and sat as still as a stone. And there I stood, waiting, and looking ridiculous, until Miss Seymour said: "Gertrude, be seated, please; we are waiting for you." Then I sat down in Prissy's seat, but I looked cross at her, and did not sing on the first line. Miss Seymour noticed it, and stopped them all, and told me if I was going to sing in the chorus, I must sing now. Then I said: "I want my own seat, Miss Seymour; I can't sing so well unless I am where I belong."

And then what did Prissy do but tell her I chose the best seat in the class and kept it from all the rest. "She wants this seat because it is by the window and she can get a breeze now and then," said Prissy. Now I thought that was so mean! I had never once thought of the window. I liked to sit there because I could get the sound of Miss Seymour's voice on the hard parts, and because I had got used to the place.

I said, "It's no such thing!" and then Miss Seymour said: "Oh, girls, don't quarrel about such a trifle as that. It doesn't matter which sits first, you or Prissy, but it does matter that we get home some time to-night."

After that the rehearsal went on. In the recess Prissy got up and said to me: "Take your seat, do, and look out of the window as much as you want to; though how it came to belong to you any more than to me, would be hard to tell."

This made me very angry, and I said: "It is my seat because I have had it at every rehearsal, and nobody has said a word. I am sure if I had known you wanted it so badly, though, I would have given it up. You might have had it without stealing."

Then Prissy would not sit down in it again, and I wouldn't. She stood before me and waited, and I wouldn't get up, and when the girls came back she took the seat below me, and that left the one at the end without a chair.

Just then Professor Mills came in to sing with us. "What is this vacant chair for?" he asked, the moment he stepped on the platform. We girls kept still, and Miss Seymour told him it belonged either to Prissy or me, but we neither of us seemed to want it. I think she might have told him that it had been mine all the time, but she didn't.

"Oh, they don't," he said, and he looked hard

at us. My face was red, I know by the feeling,
and Prissy's looked like a peony. He waited a
minute, then he said : "Hannah Smith, you may
come and occupy this seat, and keep it to-morrow."

Now Hannah Smith is the girl at the very end
of the class, and she has a little peeping voice;
it wouldn't have made a speck of difference if
she had not sung at all; and there he put her at
the head as if she were the leader! Then, there
was something worse than that. I did not think
of it until afterwards; but that changed things
so, that when we marched to the grove, I had to
walk with Hannah Smith, and Prissy had to
walk with Trudie Ellis whom she doesn't like
very well, and that disarranged all the others.
They had planned to march with their friends,
and there was the dreadfullest mix-up that you
ever saw! The girls did not like it one bit, and
they looked cross at us, and said it was a pity
that everybody had to suffer, because those two
children were silly enough to quarrel! Miss
Seymour would not let them change around at
all; she said there had been trouble enough
already made by that.

So there we were, and there we had to stay,

all through the exercises and the marching, and everything. Then, when we went up to receive our wreaths, Hannah got the one which had been made for me. I knew it in an instant. My dear Miss Dunlap sent it to me from her own lovely garden, but she had pinned on it a paper which read: " For the first right-hand girl in the procession." That was to have been me, and she knew it, and there it was Hannah. Oh dear, such a mix! Prissy did not speak to me all day long, nor I to her. Besides, I was so cross to poor Hannah that I don't think she had a bit good time. She would much rather have been down at the foot, with her friend Sarah.

The only speck of comfort I can find to-night, is the thought that there isn't anything in the verses for July, to prick into me. I have had enough to bear, and I am glad they can't sting me. There isn't any possible way of making them fit.

Monday: Oh, dear! They did fit, and pricked the worst of anything I ever had. You see, we went on quarrelling, Prissy and I, and wouldn't speak to each other in Sunday-school, and wouldn't go to the woods on Saturday. That is, I wouldn't go, because Prissy was invited, and she wouldn't go because I was, and so we both stayed at home. I don't know how father heard of it, unless Tom told him; Tom does always manage to tell things, somehow, but I am glad he did this time, for if he hadn't, I don't know how we would ever have gotten out of our trouble. It kept growing worse and worse.

Sunday night, father asked to see our verses for the month, and he read them over very carefully, then he called me, and pointed to the last one, and told me he wanted me to read it. "Thine own friend, and thy father's friend forsake not." I did, and then I asked him why he wanted me to read it, and he said it reminded him of a story he wanted to tell me.

Then he told me about a young man who got into bad company, and stayed out late nights, and began to smoke, and play cards, and even drink a little wine; and he was getting ready to break his mother's heart; but there was a man two years younger than he, who tried to help him in every way he could think of. He would help him with his work, and coax him away from bad companions, and wait for him at night, and let him in, to keep him from disgrace, and do *everything* for him.

He said sometimes he was angry with the young man for trying to help him, and would say cross and hateful things, but they were all taken patiently, and, oh, I can't tell it! It was a long story and very interesting ; I got so busy listening, that I forgot to wonder why father was telling it, or what it had to do with our verses, until after he had said that the young man succeeded at last in saving his friend, he said : " Gertrude, you know one of the men."

" I do !" I said, and I was so glad. It made it sound like a story out of a book.

" Yes," father said, " I was one of them."

I went and put my arms around father's neck and said I knew he was the good young man, that it was just like him, but he said : " No, Gertrude, I was the bad young man, and I came just as near going to ruin as many people do. I think I should have gone, but for my friend, who has been in Heaven for a good many years, but I have never forgotten him. He, Gertrude, he was your friend Prissy's father."

Then in less than a minute, I knew which verse was going to prick. Prissy's father ! and here I had been " forsaking my father's friend," or at least forsaking his own daughter which was worse! I felt dreadfully. I told father I would ask Prissy to forgive me, and make up, and love her always whatever she did, just for his sake. I made up my mind that night, that whether Prissy would speak to me or not, I would be just as good to her as I knew how. This morning as soon as I was up, I ran over to Prissy's, and went up to her room, and said: "Prissy, I want you to forgive me, and let me be your friend, because your father was my father's friend, and he says he will never forget it."

Then Prissy raised up in bed and threw both arms around me and said:

"I think I was real mean; for you ought to have had the seat, and I have been sorry ever since."

GERTRUDE'S DIARY

MY SIN IS EVER BE-
FORE ME.

HONOR THY FATHER AND
THY MOTHER; THAT THY DAYS MAY
BE LONG UPON THE LAND WHICH
THE LORD THY GOD GIVETH THEE.

WHOSO CURSETH HIS FATHER AND MOTHER, LET HIM DIE
THE DEATH.

SO THE LORD WAS ENTREATED FOR THE LAND, AND THE
PLAGUE WAS STAYED FROM ISRAEL.

THOU HAST MAGNIFIED THY WORD ABOVE ALL THY NAME.

YESTERDAY was my birthday and I had
the girls here to tea. We had a great
deal of fun, and some things that were improv-
ing. For instance, we read over our verses and
talked about them. The way we happened to do

61

that, was because Namie said she thought they were easy, this time. We asked her what she meant, and she said why, they kind of had nothing to do with us girls. We laughed at her a little. Prissy said we must remember that people who gave Namie an easy time were those who had nothing to do with her, but of course she did not mean that. Then we got to talking over the verses, and making Namie prove why they had nothing to do with us.

She said the first one was for dreadfully wicked people — murderers, and thieves, and such. That their consciences troubled them all the time. And the third one was for very wicked people too. Who but a person who was fearfully wicked would think of cursing his father and mother? Then the fourth was about a plague, and we didn't have plagues in this country; and the last one couldn't be practised, it was just a fact.

Then Ruth said, " Why, you have skipped the one that speaks right to us — ' Honor thy father and mother.' "

No, Namie said, she hadn't skipped it; but it was easy enough to do, for girls who had such fathers and mothers as we had. Of course we would honor them. We never thought of doing anything else. For her part, she thought her mother the best woman in the world. But I told her that that couldn't be, for it would not be *possible* for her to be better than my mother. Then we all got to laughing, and were real gay over it. I didn't say much, but after all, I didn't quite agree with Namie about some things. I know my conscience has spoken pretty loudly to me sometimes, and wouldn't let me study or sleep, because I had done something wrong; and I hadn't stolen anything, or murdered anybody, either; but such things are hard to explain, so I didn't try.

It was after supper that I meant to tell about. We had a real splendid supper. Mother did everything that she could to make the table look lovely.

The girls said how lovely everything was, and Namie spoke of the verse again, and said it was easy enough for us to honor our mothers, she was sure, when they took such trouble for us.

Then we went out for a walk. We were going to the lake for a row, but Ben didn't come in time, so we went down town instead. We walked away out to the long bridge, and rested

awhile, until it began to grow dark.   When we
came down Duane street, the lamps were lighted.
By that time we were getting pretty tired.   I
don't know how it is that girls most always get
so kind of wild and reckless when they are tired,
but we do.   Ruth said we better turn to Main
street, for the west end of Duane street was always dark, and she did not like to walk there.
So we came up Main, laughing and talking.   We
stopped at the postoffice, for Prissy expected a
letter by the last mail.   It wasn't quite distrib-
uted, and we had to wait.   The office was pretty
full.   I never like to wait there, but Prissy said,
"Oh, do!   There are four of us."   Charlie Porter
was there, and he is the worst tease in town.
He came over to us, and began to bother.   He
wanted to see the letter in my hand; it was
nothing but a circular that I found in my pocket,
and might have shown it to him as well as not,
only it was no concern of his, and I thought I
wouldn't.   Then he snatched at it, and I snatched
back, and in doing that I accidentally knocked
his hat off; then he caught my sleeve and said,
"Halloo! bring back that stolen property."   I
don't know how it was, but we got in a real
frolic right there in the crowd.   Ruth came to

her senses first, and said, " Do come on, girls ; " so after all, we didn't get the mail.

" Mother doesn't like us to wait in the post-office in the evening," Ruth said, as soon as we were out. " I'm sorry we waited at all."

I never heard my mother say anything about it, because I don't go to the office, Ben does that. But I knew as well as anything that she wouldn't have liked it.

I should have thought that we would have sobered down after that, but Prissy was in a real frolic.

" Let's have some fun," she said. " Let's go into the drug store here, and get some soda."

She has a cousin who is clerk in the store, and we sometimes go there. Ruth held back, but Prissy coaxed and said she had twenty cents to spend as she liked, and it was burning a hole in her pocket, and she was dreadfully thirsty. So at last we went. There were a good many people there; among them a young man who used to board at Prissy's. He came over where we were and began to frolic with us, and we talked and laughed, and had just the gayest time! I didn't think how late it was getting and none of us did, until just as we were going out. Dick — that is the young man — asked us to wait a minute; that he had a package he wanted Prissy to take to her brother. We stood in the door and waited, and we were laughing then, over some of the funny things Dick had said; but we heard a man in the back part of the store say:

"Who are those girls?"

His voice sounded real gruff. I turned around and looked at him, but I didn't know him. The clerk answered:

"Oh, they are some of our townspeople."

"Well, they must have queer mothers!" This was what the gruff voice said next, and I tell you we girls were still enough. We looked at one another and wondered if he could possibly mean us, and we didn't speak a word.

He did, though. "I have been watching them," he said; "I never saw properly brought up girls act so badly on the street. They have been in the postoffice, talking loud, and shouting with laughter, and romping with a young fellow there; and now they are doing the same thing here. It isn't possible that they have been properly taught, or they would not behave like that on the street. If they have respectable

mothers they ought to know that their daughters
are disgracing them."

Only think of it! O, Journal, if you *could*
think, sometimes it would be a great comfort
to me! We stood still and looked at one another. Our cheeks were as red as blush roses;
mine burned like fire, away out to my ears.
Dick hadn't come back yet, so we couldn't rush
out as we felt like doing.

"He can't mean us?" Prissy whispered, and
her teeth chattered.

"Yes, he does mean us," said Namie. "Mean
old fellow that he is. Our *mothers*, indeed!
Only think of it!"

Someway that seemed to make every one of
us think of the verse that we had decided was so
easy. I looked at Ruth and she looked at me.
" Honor thy father and "— I said, and then
stopped.

"Yes," exclaimed Ruth, "I should think as
much!"

Then she walked right across that drug store
like a queen and marched up to the man.

"I want to tell you, sir," she said, "that you
are mistaken. We have good mothers, who
have taught us how to act. We just got into a

frolic and forgot ; but you need not blame them, sir, not one bit, for they would be as sorry as you are."

Then she walked away before that astonished man could say a word.

We all marched out the next minute, and we all talked at once when we reached the street. We said that was a horrid old man, and he ought to be ashamed of himself, and we were glad Ruth told him the truth. But at last Ruth said :

"Girls, he told the truth, too; we did disgrace our mothers. They wouldn't have liked the way we have acted ever since we started out."

Well, we went home, every one of us. And we all told our mothers every bit about it. We said we would. Mine cried a little, and said she was shocked and sorry. But she kissed me and said she was glad I had told her. And she promised to expect me to honor her after this. I guess I shall be more careful than I have been. I don't believe there is a verse in the Bible but what fits us girls.

THE LORD IS MY LIGHT AND MY SALVATION: WHOM SHALL I FEAR? I DELIGHT TO DO THY WILL, O MY GOD.

BLESS THE LORD, O MY SOUL, AND FORGET NOT ALL HIS BENEFITS.

WE girls have had a real nice time, and made ten dollars for the mission box besides. Not but what some of the older ones helped us, but then, Mr. Neale says we did the most of the work, and ought to have the credit. We did a good deal of the thinking, too. That is, we put the thoughts of a good many people together, and the thing grew. It began by Prissy humming that anthem,

> Forget not, forget not, forget not
> All his benefits.

The music repeats, I don't know how many times, and Prissy was always humming it. Ruth said there was no danger of our forgetting the words at least.

Alice Burnham heard us talking about it, and she said they sang that anthem at their Thanksgiving entertainment in Rochester last fall, and had a monument built of fruits and vegetables; the base was made of moss, and had letters made of white flowers, which said,

ALL HIS BENEFITS.

"How pretty that must have been!" Ruth said; and then in a minute more she said, "I wish we could get up something pretty."

That afternoon little Essie Morgan came skipping through the hall, singing,

> Praise him, praise him, all ye little children.

That is a new song they were beginning to learn in the primary class.

"What a sweet voice that little thing has!" Prissy said, "I wish we could get up something pretty in the Sunday-school and have her sing. There are ever so many of those little things who sing nicely."

" Yes," Namie said. " There is Gertie Scanlon, she has a sweet voice. Wouldn't it be nice, girls, if we could get up something and put her in it, and get her father to come to church and hear her?"

Well, that was the beginning, and it was queer to see how the thing grew. We girls went to see Mr. Neale, and he liked it ever so much. He always does like things. And he helped us. We had the entertainment in our chapel last night, and everybody says it was lovely.

Alice Burnham declares that it was ever so much prettier than the one they had in Rochester, and not a bit like it.

Mr. Robinson was the one who helped us most. He made all the blocks for the monument. Then he had to come, to see how they worked, and Mr. Neale says it is the first time he has been inside of a church in ten years. Rob Chandler painted the letters for us.

First, we had a base, like that Alice Burnham told us of. He made that part just like hers — moss, and flowers, and all, and it was just lovely.

The letters shone like stars out of the green moss —

ALL HIS BENEFITS.

You could see them all over the church.

Then we had each little girl come up and bring a white marble block lettered with black. At least it was painted wood, but it looked like marble.

The first one was LIFE. And the one above it was HOME. Each block was a little shorter than the one below it, and they fitted nicely, and when they were done they were just the shape of a pyramid. Each little girl recited a Bible verse, or a verse of a hymn, about the word she was bringing up. Some of the recitations were just lovely.

When Gertie Scanlon brought up her block, and it had on it FATHER, and recited, *Like as a father pitieth his children, so the Lord pitieth them that fear him,* they said that Philip Scanlon put down his head and cried. He is truly a good father now, since he stopped drinking.

There were ever so many blocks, and at the last, we put a lovely cross, and the girls all recited : *He gave his life a ransom for many.*

Then the little children all marched around, singing,

Praise him, praise him, all ye little children.

Each one stopped before the cross, and held up a bouquet of flowers, and Alice Burnham took them and put them in the cross. It was covered with bright red paper, but bored into the wood, under the paper, were little holes, through which the flowers were pushed; and when the children had all brought bouquets, the cross had blossomed out into flowers. It was the prettiest thing I ever saw. The last verse of the song is,

Crown him, crown him, all ye little children.

Each of the little ones had a wreath of flowers, and as they sang that verse, marching, they hung their wreaths on the cross, or dropped them at its base. Everybody was as pleased as they could be. Ruth says she thinks our verses helped us this month, anyway. We girls, and the boys from Mr. Stuart's class, sang the anthem, *All His Benefits*, and they say we sang it very well.

We took up a collection for the Mission Band, to which all the little ones belong, and got twenty dollars. So then half was voted to our Band, and half to the little children.

I don't know when we have had nicer times than in getting this up. Mother says she is proud of us because we did it without any jars.

GERTRUDE'S DIARY

AND THOU, SOLOMON, MY SON, KNOW THOU THE GOD OF THY FATHER, AND SERVE HIM WITH A PERFECT HEART, AND WITH A WILLING MIND.

ARISE, THEREFORE, AND BE DOING, AND THE LORD BE WITH THEE.

WISDOM IS THE PRINCIPAL THING, THEREFORE GET WISDOM.

MINE HOUSE SHALL BE CALLED AN HOUSE OF PRAYER.

OH dear, oh dear! I didn't think I would ever write in my diary when I felt so sorrowful as I do to-night. I have just made a great blot on the paper, but I cannot help it, the tears won't stay back. I am not going to write here any more. I can't write in any book

75

for awhile, and I am sure I cannot ever write
in this one again : I am just going to shut it up
and lay it away. I don't want to burn it, for
it has father's name in it a good deal.

Just to think how everything can change in
one little month! Last month I had a birthday party and was so merry. It doesn t seem
to me as though I could ever be merry again.

We are going away from Locust Shade.
Going to the city to live. We four girls who
have been together all our lives are to be sep-
arated. They all stay here and have good times,
but I am to go away to a great lonely city. We
are poor now, and I can't go to school any more.
At least, not now. Ben says he is going to
work, and earn money, and take care of us, and
in a little while I can go again. But Ben is
only a boy.

He is all we have now, though. Dear father
is gone. God called him away to Heaven
almost two weeks ago : it seems like two years.
Oh, but I ought not to cry so much. I do try
to be cheerful when I am down-stairs. When
I can't stand it any longer, I rush away up here
and cry alone. Our B. R. N. Society is broken
up. Or no, not broken up, either, for I have

promised to go right on and have a reading all
by myself, and try to mind the verses, and all
that, but it will be very different.

I shall try, though, to do it, for I do think the
verses have helped me. And this month they
are just wonderful! That first one was what
father said to Ben just two days before he died.
I was studying the verse, and father called me
and asked me to say it slowly to him. Then
when Ben came in he called him and repeated
it to him, very solemnly, putting his name in
the place of Solomon. "And thou, Benjamin
my son, know thou the God of thy father, and
serve him with a perfect heart, and with a willing mind. I can't leave you any better word
than that," father said. "I hope you will serve
him ten times better than your father has, and
always with a willing mind. Then we shall
meet in Heaven and talk it all over." He said
a good deal more; and Ben cried. But I don't
believe he will ever forget that verse.

My verse is just as wonderful. The next day
father talked with me about how I must be
brave and strong, and help mother all I could.

"You are the oldest daughter at home," he
said, "and mother must learn to depend on

you. There are ever so many ways in which
you will find that you can help her. Here is
my good-by message, and I hope you will never
forget it. 'Arise, therefore, and be doing, and
the Lord be with thee.'"

I tried hard to keep back the tears, so I
could hear every word that father said, and he
talked *so* beautifully to me! He said I was to
call that verse mine, and that whenever I fel*
like sitting down and crying, and being dis
couraged, I must think of him saying to me
"Arise, therefore, and be doing, and the Lord
be with thee." It is that verse which has
helped me so much during these two sad weeks.
Mother says I have been a comfort to her.
That she did not know I could help her about
so many things. I guess I have said over
those words twenty times in an hour, some days.
Ben says he is just so.

"I tell you what, Gertrude," he said to me
last night, "you and I have business before us, if
we live up to those two verses. There will be
no chance to sit down and mope. And father
will be disappointed if we don't live them."
So we are going to try, Ben and I, as hard as
ever we can. But I don't mean to write in this

journal any more. It makes me cry. It is too much mixed up with the happy days when I was a little girl. I don't feel like a little girl now.

This evening mother and I had a long talk. I told her about Ben's verse, and mine. She cried a good deal, but she did not look very unhappy. She kissed me and said father had left a fortune to us. That it would save Ben and me for this life, and for Heaven if we followed his directions. Then she asked for my verses and studied them quite awhile, and said, "I think, Gertrude, I will take this for mine: 'Mine house shall be called an house of prayer.' We will try in our new home not to do anything, or say anything, or even *think* anything that we cannot speak to God about and ask his help."

So now we have each of us a verse; only mother has another, a special one. She says this is her house verse, but that father left one for her own private help. That some day perhaps she will tell me what it is, but she wants to keep it to herself now.

To-morrow we are going away. Mother is to be forewoman in a ladies' store. How very

strange that seems! I am to be one of the cash
girls, and learn how to make ˌtrimming, and
crochet work. Ben is to go into another store.
The girls are just as kind as they can be. They
say they will write to me every week, and tell
me all about the school, and the Sabbath-school,
and every thing. I have promised to write a
letter something like a journal to them, telling
them about things and how the verses match,
what happens to me, and all that.

We have a good many plans, but it seems as
though nothing was real sure any more. Only
this: I belong to Jesus Christ, and am going
to "arise" and "be doing" everything that I
think he would like to have me. Then, some
day, we are all going home to Heaven, to be
with father. When I see him I want to be able
to say: "Father, I did it all, as well as I could."
Good-by old journal! I am sorry for many
things I have said to you: but you have some
nice times, and some dear names, and some
good verses to take care of.

PART ONE.

IT began by Anna Maylie saying "Oh dear!" as many as five times in the course of one half-hour. At the end of every "oh dear," she yawned as though she might possibly be tired of life. Her aunt Sarah looked up at last from the letter she was writing. "Have you really nothing to do?" she asked. Whereupon Anna laughed and looked a little ashamed. "I've plenty to do," she said, "but I don't want to do it. Aunt Sarah, I'm so tired of everything we have ever done; I wish we could have something different."

"Modest wish!" said aunt Sarah, but she dried her pen, a signal for Anna to talk.

"Well, I do, anyhow. There isn't anything nice for young boys and girls to do evenings. Those older ones have their C. L. S. C. and real good times going to it, and getting ready for it.

And the silly ones have their dancing club every two weeks; but for us, Tom, and Mary, and Cora, and John and the rest of us, there isn't a thing to do. I thought about a cooking-club such as those Tu-Whit Hollow girls had, you know, but we couldn't do it; our mothers wouldn't let us; and besides, the boys couldn't help very well, and there are more boys than girls of us cousins, and the Burkes are as good as cousins — we are always together — and they are all boys, you know. Aunt Sarah, couldn't you think of something nice and new? You always think such good things."

Anna had reached a period now, and said the thing that most of all she wanted to say. Aunt Sarah laughed, but at once put on a thoughtful look, and asked questions as to the ages and scholarship of the numerous cousins and friends whose acquaintance she was making this winter, and ended by promising to think the matter over and report.

"And she will think something splendid," explained Anna to the cousins, next day, "you see if she doesn't, when aunt Sarah goes to thinking, something comes of it." In less than a week from that time there was much excitement among the young people as they met to talk up the idea that aunt Sarah had thought out.

"A history class!" did John exclaim. "Why, I thought it was to be fun; that looks like work."

"There is always a lot of work about every kind of fun," said philosopher Tom. "I suppose this has got to be worked up first, and the fun comes in afterwards."

"The fun comes in the guessing," said Anna. "You needn't be in the first work, John, you may be the audience and do the guessing."

"I don't understand it at all," complained Cora. "Let's get aunt Sarah to come in and explain it to us."

And they did. It took a great many words, and a great many interruptions in the shape of questions, before the eager young people understood; but I can tell you about it in fewer words than aunt Sarah used. The plan was to have a Society, or a Circle, or a "Cube" — as Anna proposed that they call themselves — in order to have something new, and meet each month. A committee from their number was to be appointed each month by the President, to prepare the entertainment for the next meeting, and this committee were to prepare some fact in connection with the history of our own country, and present it in any shape they could, while the duty of the others was to guess what they were talking about. On her part, aunt Sarah promised to help each committee, which was to be so varied as to include all the members in regular routine. The scheme suited the young people wonderfully well. The only fault they found was with the proposal to meet only once a month. But in this aunt Sarah was inexorable: "Your committee will need every bit of that time to prepare their work," she explained. "Tom never spoke a truer word than when he said that all fun, at least all fun that amounts to anything, has to be preceded by a good deal of work."

"Yes, but what are the rest of us fellows going to do while the committee are getting ready?" growled John, who never really growled, but always argued every inch of his way.

"Plenty of things; get your President to appoint a committee for the next month, and hold corner meetings, making out your plans, and then do your working up, at home, in your leisure moments."

A President was the next thing in order, and to John's great surprise, he was unanimously chosen, aunt Sarah proposing that they should depart from the usual custom of societies, by allowing the officers to take their turns in the entertainments : appointing a President pro tem, for the night, the regular officer was engaged.

"Now what," said Cora, "is a President pro tem ? The C. L. S. C. folks elected him the other night at our house, and I wondered then, but there was nobody to ask who wouldn't laugh at me for being a dunce."

It is well she said that, for Tom was all ready to laugh; instead he said gravely, "Ahem! President John, air your Latin for my little sister's benefit." And John in a very gentle tone explained : "*Pro Tempore* are the Latin words which mean 'for the time being,' Cora; and so when we want a President, or any sort of officer just for a little while until the regular one is ready, we say President pro tempore, or pro tem, for short."

"Oh," said Cora, "that is easy enough to understand."

"Cora is a little young for our society," whispered Anna to Helen Banks, "but then she would feel dreadfully to be left out, and I suppose they had children around them in those old times." To this supposition, Helen gravely assented. Then Tom had another question to settle: "What about a name? We must call ourselves something, and have a plan to vote members in, and all that. Who are to belong, anyway?"

"Who are to be the organic members, I suppose you mean."

"Let's count," said Anna; "there are thirteen of us cousins, to begin with. Isn't it funny to have so many of us all living in the same town?"

"Some of us are rather young," said Tom significantly.

"Oh, I know, but then we must all belong; we don't want to divide the family. Then there are the Burkes, of course they'll belong."

"And Harry and Ralph Whiting," said Tom.

"And Kate Whiting too, then."

"Well, if we have the Whitings I think we ought to have the Goldens, for they are their cousins, and they always go together. And the Percivals live just next door to us, and are in and out so much, we most ought to have them."

A low whistle from Tom at this point, arrested attention: "What?" said President John.

"Why, have you been counting names? Exactly twenty-seven; here are we three in this house, and you three in yours, and the three Pinkham cousins — three times three are nine — and the little cousins and the outsiders, make three times nine, exactly twenty-seven; a cube!"

"That's a fact," said John; "we've got a name; we'll call ourselves Cube Root."

"That is worse than Pro Tem," said Cora in dismay. Tom tried to explain: "Twenty-seven is the cube of three, little girl."

"Is the what!" said Cora; then they all laughed; and President John said encouragingly: "Never mind, Cora, you will learn."

And they all voted to call themselves "The Cube."

PART II.

Great was the flutter among the cousins on the evening in which The Cube was to have its first meeting. Mrs. Maylie's large sitting-room had been given up all day to the committee, and they performed there with closed doors. When, at seven o'clock, the other members of The Cube began to arrive, the door was unlocked, but a long green calico curtain had been stretched across the upper half of the room, behind which much giggling could be heard, while fantastic shadows danced about on the curtain, to the great delight of the audience.

At last Cora drew back the curtain, and a murmur of satisfaction was heard in the room. The south end of the sitting-room was certainly a very pretty spot. The bay window was filled with plants and flowers. Baskets of roses from Mr. Bryan's conservatory filled the air with perfume. A tuberose was growing and blooming in one corner, the great oleander-tree had been moved from the upper hall, and stood in the centre of the space, and smaller plants, with broad green leaves, were set around it in a way to form a sort of bower. Within this pretty spot was evidently a fountain; to be sure it was nothing but the baby's bath-tub, hidden by the plants, and Anna Maylie, hidden from view by an ingenious arrangement of green curtain trimmed with evergeen, steadily poured tiny gurgling streams of water from a hidden flower-sprinkler. Beside the fountain stood a little gray-haired, wrinkled old man, an expression of disappointment and gloom on his old face. He was dressed in a very peculiar costume, which the audience studied carefully, trying to decide of what nation he might be. Other little men were around him, dressed also in bright, quaint colors, and in the background stood a richly painted and feather-decked Indian.

"How far over the waters come you?" asked the Indian in surprisingly good English.

One of the old man's attendants answered for him:

"We come from across much waters; away from the sunny islands in the Atlantic Ocean. This man"—laying his hand familiarly on the gray headed man's shoulder—"is the chief of the island from whence we come."

"The mischief he is," said President John from the audience, speaking in a low voice to Ralph Whiting; "then that puts me all awry in my guess. If he isn't dressed in Spanish costume, I don't know that costume when I see it."

"Well," whispered Ralph, "some of those old Spaniards went out to the West Indies; I suppose they kept their home dress."

"Hark!" said John. "Look at him!" For the Spaniard, if Spaniard he were, had stooped, and was taking a long, slow draught of water from the tinkling fountain. "It is not true," he said, slowly and sadly, shaking his gray head, "it is not true what those adventurers told me; I have been everywhere, and drank of the waters, and I do not find it; the waters are sweet and good, but what they said is not to be found. I must go back to my island a disappointed man."

"He speaks surprisingly good English," murmured several of the audience.

"What is he hunting after?" asked Fannie Burke. "John, what was that story about a Spaniard hunting for gold or something?"

"They went to South America for gold," said John; "but he seems to have come *away* from somewhere, to the United States."

Then they listened again; but the talk, though really very interesting, was rather obscure, except that they gathered that the travellers knew much about Spain, and at last they plainly referred to that country as their home. At the same time they addressed the old man as Governor, and all the time he expressed by word, or act, disappointment; every few moments he would take another sip of the water, and shake his head.

"This is a beautiful flowery country," said one of the Spaniards, looking around admiringly on the plants and flowers.

"Ah, that it is!" assented the Governor, and this is *Pasqua de Flores*, is it not?"

"Ah, ha!" said President John, and he nodded his head eagerly at his particular friend Ralph. "They'll name the spot next," he whispered, "and take possession of it in the name of the King of Spain."

"What is Pasqua de Flores?" whispered Kate Whiting.

"Why, it is Flowery Easter; that is what the Spaniards used to call it; now if we could remember who landed in this country on Easter Sunday, we'd have them."

Another drink of water, a few words together, and the Governor, raising a cup of sparkling water, and sprinkling it about the flowers, said in slow, pompous tones, "I take possession of this country in the name of the King of Spain, and name it "— he waited a reasonable length of time according to promise, for any of the audience who could supply the name, and then added — "FLORIDA." A clapping of hands from the audience followed.

More drinks of water ; the Governor was certainly very thirsty ; but it did not seem to make him happy. Sadly he shook his head. "It is a failure," he said, bowing himself nearly to the floor to express his deep disappointment. "I shall have to return to my country a disappointed, deceived old man, with the gray hairs and the wrinkles still gaining on me."

A tremendous clapping of hands from the audience, and President John sprang up : "Give me leave," he said, " to introduce Ponce de Leon, Governor of Porto Rico, who has failed in his search for the fountain which was to make him young again, but has found and named the beautiful country of Florida."

Then what shouting, and clapping, and chattering! Those who did not know the story of Ponce de Leon, wanted to hear it at once, and were directed to ask Ponce de Leon himself, for who should know better than he, the story of his life. So they questioned him, and I must say he told it well.

After that the committee and audience chatted together as boys and girls, and ate apples, and talked over their trials in getting ready for the entertainment, and voted the first meeting of The Cube a great success.

"Only," said little Cora, "I can't help being sorry for poor Ponce de Leon, he wanted to be young again so badly, and nobody told him how he could."

"How he could?" said President John curiously. "Why, Cora, you don't know of a way, do you?"

"Of course I do. You don't suppose he would be an old man in Heaven, do you?"

"Oh!" said President John.

PART III.

The committee laughed so much over their queer dresses that at one time it seemed as though they would never get ready to have the curtain drawn.

"Kate can never make herself look like a Dutch lady," said John. "She is too tall and thin."

"I don't believe the Dutch ladies appeared on this occasion," said Kate, looking down at her thick boots and short dress, which, however, seemed a long dress to her.

"Don't you think it! They were hovering around somewhere; anyhow, they ought to have been. How could a peace be patched up unless the women were in it?"

"I don't believe they will ever guess the scene," said Fannie Burke complacently. She knew she made a nice little German.

"Come on, Charlie!" said Ralph. "Push back the curtain; aren't we ready, John?"

In two minutes more they appeared before their eager audience, a goodly company of Dutchmen, in their knee breeches and broad hats, the women with bare heads and short, straight dresses, and stout shoes. They formed a half-circle, which was made complete by five of as fierce-looking Indians as one need wish to see. It is wonderful how quickly a little cheap paint, a few feathers, and some bright colors, will make peaceful American boys into Iroquois Indians! What was that long bright thing they held in their hands, the Indian chief holding one end and the chief Dutchman the other? It was Kate Burke's scarf, that was plain to be seen; that is, it was before the Indians and Dutch got hold of it. But what was it now? They stood very near a singular-looking mound, which Grace and Mary West recognized as the large tub in which their mother's lemon-tree used to grow before the frost killed it; but its sides were so strewn with moss and lichen that the others could not decide what it was. What was that Dutchman about, bending over it? Digging a hole, as sure as the world! Was he making a grave? Yes, surely, a long deep hole, skilfully dug, and behold, the Indian chief bent his feather-decked head and laid within it a hatchet; then both Indian and Dutchman gravely covered it with earth, the two chief men, meantime, holding the scarf. What did it all mean?

"I know," said Mary, and in her eagerness she almost spoke the words aloud; "O, girls, I know. They have buried the hatchet together; that means that they will have no more war; they are holding the belt of peace."

It seemed probable that Mary's history was correct, for just then the two leaders raised their arms, and each Dutchman and savage walked slowly and solemnly under the belt; then forming a circle, clasping hands, and each taking hold of the belt, the circle of peace was complete.

"Is that the way the Indians did?" whispered Cora.

"I don't know," said Mary. "It's pretty, isn't it? I know they buried the hatchet. I've read about it often."

"But where is all this taking place?" asked Tom Maylie· "that's what *I* want to get at."

However, they did not get at it, any of them; not even after one of the Dutchmen brought out a great signboard, on which were painted in good-sized letters, the words: "NEW NETHER-LANDS." In fact, it was not until the Indian chief and the chief Dutchman had shaken hands, and the Dutchman had assured the chief that Hendrick Christiansen would never forget the promise made that day, nor the circle formed with the belt of peace, that the audience was sure of their ground.

"What dunces we are!" Tom Maylie said in intense disgust. "Now I knew perfectly well that that old Dutchman, Christiansen, sailed up

the Hudson and built a fort, and made peace
with the Indians."

"So did I," said Mary Burke; "after they
told me, I knew all about it!"

But there was not much time for talk, for the
curtain which had been drawn after the hand-
shaking, was pushed back again, and here were
Indians again, more of them; and more Dutchmen, women in their Dutch dresses, and squaws
in their blankets; one even had a pappoose
strapped on her back.

"It is Nina's doll!" Mary Burke explained.
"They wanted the baby, but aunt Fannie
wouldn't let them have him."

Trading. Something was being bought, and
the Indians were being paid in beads, and bits
of red flannel, and buttons, and pieces of colored
glass. There was another leader this time, as
Dutch as Hendrick Christiansen, but not the
same man. Who was he? What was he trying to buy? A Dutchman, with pencil and
paper, kept careful count of the trades, though
lively bargains were going on all around him.
At last he reported that twenty-four dollars'
worth of beads and buttons, and the like trea-
sures, had been bought, and the governor de-

cided that that was certainly a very good price,
and the Indian chief nodded his head and
agreed to the bargain. "And now," said the
Dutchman, "Indian must remember that the
whole island is mine; I have bought it and paid
for it, and Indian must not disturb my people."

"Oh, my!" said Cora. "He has bought a
whole island for twenty-four dollars! Where
can it be?" But half a dozen voices of the
history scholars were by this time calling out:
"Manhattan, Manhattan!" and "How are you,
Peter Minuet? How did you leave the good
people in Holland?"

"I didn't know before that you took so many
men and women with you to carry out the bargain," said Tom Maylie to Peter Minuet, his
eyes dancing with fun. "You even let the
squaws help, didn't you?"

"Well," said Governor Minuet, "they wanted
to pick out their trinkets, and our women wanted
to help them, so we thought it would do no harm."

"But I want to know," said Cora, "did you
—did they really and truly buy a whole island
for twenty-four dollars?"

"We really and truly did," declared Governor Minuet. "Have you any fault to find?"

And Cora, looking sober, admitted that she did not think it was right. It might be right enough to *play* it, but if it was truly history, she thought all the Dutch ought to be sorry and ashamed.

"On the contrary," aunt Sarah said, "they had a chance to be proud; so many of the early settlers simply stole away or fought away the land from the Indians and gave them nothing in return."

"But, aunt Sarah, beads and buttons and things are just as good as nothing. Because the Indians did not know any better, was it right to cheat them?"

She was not sure that it was cheating them, aunt Sarah said, "Any more than you cheated the baby this morning, when you gave him a bit of red flannel instead of that bright silk handkerchief. The handkerchief was worth no more to baby than the red flannel; and the flannel gave him as much pleasure."

THE CUBE.

PART FOUR

NOTHING like the excitement which now prevailed had been seen among The Cubes before. Mrs. Whiting's schoolroom where they were to meet was pretty well filled by seven o'clock in the evening, with fathers and mothers and aunts and cousins and friends who had been invited. The movements of those among the Cubes who were going to perform had been so mysterious all the week, and there had been so much giggling when they met, that great curiosity had been excited to see what they were going to do. They had begged for the schoolroom, because the platform was "just the thing."

Precisely at seven o'clock the green calico curtain was drawn back, and behold! there was little Freddy Maylie in his new kilt suit, gravely drawing his express wagon across the stage, in

which sat two solemn rows of tin soldiers with
their swords by their sides! Just behind them
walked two boys in blue-belted blouses, axes
over their shoulders; two more just behind them,
one with a rake, another with a pitchfork!
Then appeared a second express-wagon, drawn
by ten tin horses that had been borrowed at
uncle Ned's toy-store, and the eager people who
were watching leaned forward to discover that
the load on the wagon was an immense loaf of
bread, the largest certainly that had ever been
baked in the Whiting kitchen.

What a large company of people there seemed
to be on that stage! They kept filing in, boys
and girls, with all sorts of tools for doing all
sorts of things, carried high in air as though
they were proud of them. In the excitement,
it took the audience some minutes to discover
that the same boys appeared again and again,
passing out of one door and evidently scamper-
ing back by the way of the hall, to seize a hoe,
or a fork, or a gun, and join the procession.

Still they came, and still the audience exclaimed and wondered. Not a word was
spoken. What could it all mean!

Behold, here was a good-sized barrel being

trundled by on a wheelbarrow, and on either side of it were two boys pounding away with all their might. Then came ten boys — no, thirteen — each carrying a great wax candle. Ten of the candles were lighted, but three were not.

"Oh, ho!" said John West, "I begin to know a thing or two."

"Well, I don't!" said Fannie Burke. "I haven't the least idea what they are about. I hope they won't set the house on fire. Why do you suppose three of those candles are left unlighted?"

"You might as well ask why ten of them are lighted," laughed John. "I guess I could answer both questions, but I don't suppose it would be fair. Look! There's Dick's printing-press being wheeled by; and there's the wheel-barrow again with a house on it — little Tim's building blocks! Look at the pillars in front! One, two, three, ten of them! I thought so."

"But tell me why," said Fannie impatiently. "Of course it would be fair to tell. You ought to help your side, and here we are, not guessing at all. I never saw anything so funny. It seems as though there were crowds and crowds of them; and there are just thirteen in all. I don't see how they get around through the back hall so quick to come in again; and they take time to put on other things too. Do tell me what they are about, John West!"

"Well, just you wait," said John, "until I am certain, besides being sure. Hold on! there's something printed on those ten pillars. When t-h-r-e-e m-o-r-e," he said, spelling out the letters as the block-house moved slowly across the stage. "I wonder how they did that. Tom printed the letters with his stencils, didn't he? then they pasted them on the blocks:

> When three more pillars rise,
> Our Union will the world surprise.

"Why, Fannie, don't you guess yet? Don't you know about the wonderful procession in New York, that time the three States, New York among them, wouldn't vote for the Constitution? They had a procession miles long, you know, with all the trades, and everything in it. Let's tell them we've guessed. Halloo!" he shouted, "we'll vote for it. You can put up your other pillars. Look, there's a flag!"

"Yes," said Fannie, "and it says, 'United we stand, divided we fall.' John, I remember it all now; but isn't it pretty? I wonder if the rest understand? Oh, hark! what's that?"

The utmost stillness all through the room; behind the curtain somewhere Ralph Whiting's toy cannon was firing.

One, two, three, four! The audience grew excited counting.

"I know how many there will be," whispered John. "Six, seven—you see if there aren't thirteen! Where's aunt Sarah? Oh, I know something so nice to do!"

"There she is sitting by the piano."

"Oh, good!"

And John West slipped through the room to her side. A few seconds of eager whispering while the cannon fired, and just as it reached its thirteenth tiny peal, aunt Sarah, turning to the piano, struck merrily into the little Spanish song that the Cubes had all been practising in school to sing in the "Historic Tableau of all Nations."

Then the audience cheered. For by this time all who remembered anything about the early beginnings of freedom, remembered that a Spanish ship lying in the New York harbor was the first to salute the New World with thirteen guns, one for each State.

PART FIVE.

NEW plans were adopted at their next meeting. Those in whose hands the entertainment was, reported that their ideas were so large they would need the help of every member of the Cube, and that the audience must be made up entirely of invited guests.

Everybody was delighted with this, for, pleasant as it was to sit and listen, of course it was ever so much nicer to be one of the performers; so preparations went on rapidly.

Anna Maylie rushed in from school to tell her mother about it. And now Mrs. Maylie had a great deal to do. In their family it happened that the grandmother, and the grown-up son, and Neddie, aged two, had a birthday to celebrate on the very same day of the month, though there was some difference in their ages. This triple festival always gave the Maylie fam-

ily an excuse for having a great time : and the
Cubes were delighted to remember that
the festival fell in the month of May. They
changed the evening of their entertainment to

THE GRANDMOTHER.

match the day, and Mrs. Maylie took hold
of matters with energy. By six o'clock the
schoolroom was in order, or disorder, just as
you were pleased to consider it, and the

guests were seated. Then the curtain was drawn.

What a curious moving tableau! What was *not* going on? Two of the girls were hurriedly picking the feathers from a great turkey, and a pair of plump chickens. Anna Maylie was putting flour and fruit and butter and eggs together in a way that suggested to wise people an old-fashioned plum pudding. Harry and Ralph were cracking nuts. Tom was shelling corn into a popper, Kate Whiting was peeling apples, and somebody else was rolling pie crust, and somebody else was chopping mince meat. Lucy Pinkham was filling lovely little tarts, and in short, almost everything you can think of that has to do with getting up a splendid dinner, was going on among those young people. Every one of them was hurrying as though the time for preparation was very short, and the big white aprons and tucked-up dresses, and rolled-up sleeves, and quick movements and comical expressions, all made a very funny as well as a-very pretty picture. The guests clapped their hands heartily, and insisted on seeing the tableau again and yet again. One of them said that a nice supper was certainly being prepared, and she only hoped that whatever its name was, she should get invited to help it.

After the curtain was drawn for the third time, a great deal of scurrying around and some giggling was heard behind it. Meantime the guests chatted pleasantly together and waited. When it was drawn back once more, things had greatly changed. Behold rows and rows of people in odd old-fashioned bonnets and coats, the boys on one side, the girls on the other, seated in rows, while in a high pulpit stood John, hymn book in hand, having evidently just given out the hymn, and Ralph in a swallow-tailed coat, and his grandfather's tuning fork, stood ready to pitch it. It was really a very funny sight, and the audience fairly shouted with laughter over the children's success in imitating old-fashioned men and women.

Before the curtain fell, it had been fully decided that the Cube had been giving pictures of thanksgiving time in the early days. There were to be three scenes, and great was the guessing as to what the third would be. Some thought an old-fashioned wedding or quilting, or perhaps an apple-paring bee.

They waited patiently, occasionally remarking that it was very quiet behind that curtain;

the performers must be making most of their preparations in another room. Sure enough, in a little while Harry Whiting appeared and announced that for the convenience of all concerned, they had decided to have the next scene in the large room across the hall, to which all the guests were requested to go immediately.

This they did without delay. Imagine their surprise on being taken possession of the moment the door opened, by a trim little man or woman in an old-fashioned dress, and led to a seat at the great dining-table, which was spread with all the delightful old-fashioned dishes they could think of. Turkeys beautifully cooked, chicken pie, and everything else to match. Never were guests more surprised : and never, I suppose, did supper taste better. They all began to understand why Mrs. Maylie and aunt Sarah had had so much to do for the last two weeks.

Uncle Ben Whiting was heard to remark as he helped himself to a second piece of mince pie, that of all the societies for entertainment and improvement, that The Cube was ahead !

Grandma sat at the head of the table, and put sugar in everybody's coffee, her face aglow with smiles, and baby was tied into a high chair at the foot of the table, and kept everybody about him in a state of excitement as to what he would do next.

Grandma was eighty, and baby was eight months, and the grown-up grandson who sat about in the middle of the table, said he was somewhere between the two, he couldn't remember just where. Everybody was busy and happy. And the closing meeting of The Cube for the season was pronounced the best of all.

I forgot to tell you that they had voted to have no more meetings until the long winter evenings came again.

www.ingramcontent.com/pod-product-compliance
Lightning Source LLC
Chambersburg PA
CBHW022145020726
47496CB00008B/2569